THE HEIGHTS®

D1111492

SADDLEBACK
EDUCATIONAL PUBLISHING

T H E   H E I G H T S ®

Blizzard	Ransom
Camp	River
Crash	Sail
Creature	Shelter
Dam	Score
Dive	Swamp
Heist	Treasure
Jump	Tsunami
Mudslide	Twister
Neptune	**Wild**

Original text by Ed Hansen
Adapted by Mary Kate Doman

SADDLEBACK
EDUCATIONAL PUBLISHING
www.sdlback.com

ISBN-13: 978-1-61651-672-7
ISBN-10: 1-61651-672-0
eBook: 978-1-61247-376-5

Printed in U.S.A.

21 20 19 18 17   5 6 7 8 9

Chapter 1

"A trip to Africa?" Lilia asked. "Are you kidding, Dad?"

"No, I'm not kidding," Rafael said. "Africa is one of the last wild places on earth."

"I remember a lot of our trips too well," said Antonio.

"So we've had some bad trips. But we always handled it, didn't we?" Rafael asked.

"All of our trips end in disaster," Lilia replied.

"Well, I think it will be fun," Ana said. "We haven't gone on a trip in a long time."

Franco Silva was in college. But he was home for spring break.

"Well," Franco said. "I've always wanted to see Africa. I'd love to go."

"I guess I'll go too," Antonio sighed.

"Hey," Lilia added. "I'm not staying home alone. Someone has to keep Dad out of trouble."

"Great!" Rafael said. "This will be our best trip yet."

"Hey, Dad. Africa is big. Where *exactly* are we going?" asked Franco.

"Africa's the world's second largest continent. There are a lot of places we could go. But we'll fly to Nairobi, Kenya. We'll spend a few days in Serengeti National Park. Next, we'll fly to the Zambezi River. We'll stay at a lodge. We can explore the river by canoe."

"Sounds like a great plan," Ana said.

Rafael had already made the reservations months before. Everyone checked the days off on the calendar until it was time for the trip.

Ana wanted the trip to be fun. So she gave everyone a box. "Here's a gift for the trip," Ana said. Inside each box was a digital camera.

"We can have a contest," said Ana. "Let's see who can take the best picture."

"What's the prize for winning?" Antonio asked.

"Don't worry about that," Lilia laughed. "You won't win. I'm going to take the best picture."

"Well, we'll see about that," Antonio stated.

"The prize," said Ana. "Well, how about the winner decides where we go on our next vacation?"

"You're on, Mom," said Franco. He really wanted to go diving again.

It was finally time for the trip. The flight from New York to Nairobi was long. As they were landing, Lilia looked out the window. She saw a big city.

"Look at that!" Lila exclaimed. "I didn't think Nairobi would be so big."

The big jet landed. Then it sped along the runway. Soon the flight attendant announced, "Welcome to Nairobi."

"I can't believe we're finally here!" Rafael exclaimed.

"He's more excited than the kids are," Ana thought.

Chapter 2

Everyone grabbed their bags. Then
they all went through customs.

A man met the Silvas near the
exit. He was tall and blonde.

"I'm Eric Gibbons," he said.
"Your guide."

"Nice to meet you, Eric," Rafael
replied. "We're excited to begin our
adventure through the Serengeti."

"Welcome to Africa," Eric said. "Are you ready for an awesome time?"

"Oh yes," declared Antonio. "We are *so* ready."

Eric led them to a large four-wheel drive vehicle.

"This isn't the best car for the city. But it's good for the bush," said Eric.

Eric had an accent. It sounded familiar. But it didn't sound African.

"You don't sound like you're from here," Lilia said.

"Right you are," Eric said. "I'm from Australia. I came to Africa four years ago."

"What made you come here?" asked Ana.

"Well, Australia was too small for me," Eric laughed. "I want to see all seven continents. Being a guide in the Serengeti is one stop along the way."

Antonio and Lilia asked Eric about the animals in the Serengeti.

"You'll see *lots* of animals," Eric stated. "The park is loaded with predators and prey. This is the best time to visit."

The ride to camp took four hours. The Silvas were happy to get there.

Even though they had to sleep in tents, the camp was nice. The tents were set up on wooden platforms. A bed, desk, and chairs were in each tent. The tents were a lot nicer than the ones back home. Oil lamps provided light.

The kitchen was in the middle of the camp. Four African employees ran the kitchen and cooked all of the meals. The kitchen staff was kept busy with all of the tourists.

After dinner, Franco asked Eric if an animal had ever attacked him.

"We're always alert and careful," Eric answered. "Animals are unpredictable. One day one may be scared of me. The next day it may charge at me. But I've never been scared for my life. My friend Kevin has though."

"Who's Kevin?" Antonio asked.

"He's a mate back in Australia," Eric answered.

"What happened to him?" asked Antonio.

"Well," Eric said. "He was swimming. He was attacked by a

huge saltwater crocodile. It's one of the most dangerous animals on the planet! Crocs grow up to 14 feet. And they fear nothing. A big croc can tear a person or large animal apart."

"What happened to Kevin?" Lilia asked. She was scared now. "Did a croc tear him apart?"

"Well, a big croc came up under him. It clamped its teeth on Kevin's arm. It dragged him under the water. Kevin knew what was happening. Even worse, he knew what would happen next."

"What happened next?" Lilia gasped.

Eric stared back at Antonio and Lilia.

"Do you know how a crocodile tears meat off its victims?" asked Eric.

Lilia and Antonio shook their heads no. Their eyes never left Eric's face.

"The croc rolls over and over in the water," Eric said. "The spinning rips the arms and legs from the victim's body. A crocodile can easily eat the body once the limbs are off. But my mate is a smart guy. He knew what the croc's next move would be. And he knew he only had one chance. Kevin wrapped his legs and free arm around the croc. When it started spinning, Kevin's body turned with it. It took a lot of courage and strength. Kevin rolled with the croc. And it worked! It saved his arm from being torn off."

"That's horrible!" Lilia cried.

"You got that right," Eric replied. "But Kevin still had a big problem. His arm was still trapped in the croc's mouth. And the croc was six feet under!"

"How'd he get away?" Antonio wondered.

"After spinning for thirty seconds, the big croc stopped moving. He must have been frustrated," Eric said. "Kevin saw his chance. He attacked. He used his free arm to poke the croc's eye. The eyes are the only weak spot on a croc. Kevin hit the eye until the croc's jaws opened. By then Kevin's lungs were bursting.

His arm was broken too. He was bleeding badly. But he struggled to the surface. People saw the attack. They pulled Kevin aboard their boat."

Rafael was shocked. "Your friend was lucky to be rescued," Rafael said.

"He sure was," said Eric. "If not for that boat, he'd have been a goner!"

"Are there crocodiles here?" Ana asked.

"Yes," said Eric. "There are lots of crocs in the lakes and rivers. But don't worry. As long as you're in the car, you're safe."

A full moon rose over the Serengeti. The Silvas fell asleep in their tents. A big adventure awaited them.

Chapter 3

The Silvas woke at dawn. They were excited to see the Serengeti Plain.

Eric loaded the four-wheel drive with food and fresh water. The car was packed.

"Is everyone ready?" asked Eric.

"Did you guys remember your cameras?" Ana asked.

Three arms shot up in the air. Each arm held a camera.

"Okay! Okay," Ana laughed. "I get it."

Eric drove them from base camp. He explained the rules used by the guides.

"We've divided this area into six zones. Each party goes to a different zone every day," said Eric.

"So we won't see the other groups today?" Rafael asked.

Eric shook his head. "No," Eric said. "The groups will be at least twenty miles apart."

"What if there's some kind of accident?" Ana asked.

"I have a radio," Eric explained. "If we have a real problem, there's always this." Eric pointed to a gun.

Lilia's eyes grew wide.

"Have you ever used that gun?" asked Lila.

"Only twice," said Eric. "But don't worry. A shot in the air will scare an animal. It will run away. That's what happened both times I used it."

About twenty minutes later, Eric turned off the road. He headed across the Serengeti. A few minutes later they reached hilly land. Then Eric stopped on top of a big hill. Vast grasslands stretched out before them. The grasslands lasted for miles. Thousands of wild animals were below them.

"Wow!" Antonio cried out. "Are those wildebeests?"

"Yes. There are zebra down there, too. Let's take a closer look," Eric said.

Soon they were close to the herd.
But Eric pointed away from the herd.

"Now there's something not many
visitors get to see," said Eric.

Everyone looked. There was a
pride of lions lying in the grass.
All the lions were looking at the
wildebeests. The Silvas took out
their cameras.

"I think they're hungry," said
Eric. "If so, they're going to attack.
Let's watch them for a bit."

The pride had five adult females
and four cubs.

"Where are the males?" Ana asked.

"Good question," Eric said. "Only
one male lives with each pride. I'm
sure he's sleeping close by. He'll stay
there until the females make a kill.

Then he'll go in for his share of the food."

"Are the lions going to kill the wildebeests?" Lila asked.

"It sure looks like it to me," Eric answered. "Watch! See how the lions spread out? Soon a few of them will charge into the herd. Then they'll chase a young wildebeest toward the hiding lions."

Lilia made a face. "I don't think I want to see this," she said.

Antonio stared at Lilia. "You don't really want to look away, do you?" he asked.

"No," Lilia replied.

The Silvas watched in awe. Four female lions crawled toward the wildebeest. One lioness stayed to protect the cubs. The tall grass hid the lions. The wildebeests did not know they were there.

Without warning two lions charged the herd. Most of the wildebeests ran away. But three wildebeests got cut off. They ran right into the lions' trap.

Chapter 4

Four lionesses chose their prey.
Jumping up, they headed for a
lone wildebeest. The lions circled
it. The wildebeest was trapped. Its
end came quickly. One lioness bit
the wildebeest's neck. It couldn't
breathe. The struggle was over. The
wildebeest was dead.

The male lion walked toward the
kill. The other female and four cubs

followed. The five lionesses and cubs waited while the male ate. When he finished, the females and cubs fed.

"That was awesome!" Eric said. "I've been here for years. That's only the third kill I've seen."

"Oh no!" Antonio cried out. "I didn't take any pictures of the lion attack."

"Too bad," Lilia said. "I took some great pictures."

"Let me see," Antonio said.

"No way," Lilia yelled. "I'm not showing anyone my pictures until the judging."

Lilia hid her camera from Antonio. Then she scrolled through her camera. She stopped at the one of a lioness attacking the wildebeest.

"I think we have a winner!" Lilia crowed.

"Don't be so sure," Antonio yelled back. "There's a lot of time left."

There was a lot more to see on the plain. The Silvas saw giraffes, impalas, zebras, and a pack of hyenas.

Back at base camp, the Silvas talked to the other visitors. Everyone shared interesting stories. But nothing compared to the Silvas' day. Seeing the lions kill the wildebeest was amazing.

The next morning, the Silvas went to a different zone.

"We may get to see some elephants today," Eric said.

"I can't wait. Make sure you have your camera ready," Ana whispered to Antonio.

They drove for over an hour.

"We're going to pass through thick brush," said Eric. "You never know what you'll see."

About twenty minutes later Eric stopped. He pointed to the left. A huge bull elephant stood in the clearing. It was only fifty yards away.

Everyone started taking pictures of the huge bull. But Antonio was distracted. He saw a young elephant calf to the right. This was his chance to get a close-up picture. He could win the prize! Everyone was looking the other way. Antonio jumped out of the car. He snuck through the brush.

Antonio moved slowly. He was 10 yards away from the baby elephant! The little calf let out a squeal. Then its mother appeared out of nowhere. She stood between Antonio and the car.

Everyone looked at Antonio. He was in a life-or-death situation. It was bad. The mother elephant thought Antonio was going after her baby. She would trample him to death to save her calf.

Eric yelled, "Antonio walk away from the calf slowly!" Then he grabbed the gun.

The mother elephant was mad. She stomped the ground with her huge feet. She raised her trunk. Then she bellowed. It was the loudest noise

Antonio ever heard. He was terrified!
The animal weighed more than a ton.
And it stared at him with hatred.
Antonio backed away from the baby
elephant. Finally he was out of the
calf's way.

The little calf trotted back to his
mother's side. They disappeared into
the brush.

"That was a very stupid thing
you did, Antonio. You must never
leave the group again!" Eric warned.
"Understand?"

Antonio looked at Eric. He knew
what he had done was dumb.

"I guess you got a great close-
up of that baby elephant," Lilia
whispered.

Antonio looked up sadly. "I almost did," he said. "But all I could think of was getting away!"

All of the Silvas laughed. Franco gathered everyone in a group.

"Come on Antonio," Franco said. "Take our picture. We won't attack you. I promise!"

Chapter 5

It was time to leave the Serengeti. The Zambezi River was the next stop. The huge river passed through six countries. The Silvas couldn't wait to get there. They'd see animals they hadn't seen in the Serengeti. After breakfast they climbed into the four-wheel drive for the last time.

After saying good-bye to Eric, the Silvas boarded a small seaplane. They flew one thousand feet over the African jungle.

"The Zambezi will be a different experience than the Serengeti," Rafael said.

"What do you mean?" asked Lilia.

"We'll be traveling on the river. And we'll see different animals," Rafael replied.

"Like what?" Franco asked.

"Hippos, crocodiles, and buffalo," said Rafael.

"Hey, Antonio," Lilia said. "This may be your big chance. Maybe you can finally take a picture of something other than us."

"Very funny," Antonio said.

Soon, the pilot called out, "Look! The Zambezi is up ahead. We'll land in twenty minutes."

The little plane followed the river downstream. The Silvas were surprised at the size of the river. It was more than a mile across in some spots.

Then the pilot spoke again. "Look! A big herd of elephants is crossing the river. I'll fly lower so you can see."

The pilot turned the plane to the right. Antonio had the best view. He quickly took pictures of the elephants swimming. Moments later the plane touched down in the river.

The Red Cliff Lodge was nice. It wasn't fancy, but it was clean and cozy. They met their new guide. He was from Rwanda. His name was Samuel. The Silvas settled into their rooms. Soon it was time for dinner. They ate in the dining room.

Franco noticed Antonio looked strange. He wondered if something was bothering him.

"Hey, Antonio," Franco said. "How'd your pictures of the elephants turn out?"

Antonio looked at Franco. He shook his head slowly.

"What's wrong?" Ana asked.

"Well, I took great pictures of the elephants," Antonio said. "But my finger was in the way. The pictures are ruined."

Lilia laughed. "It looks like you're out of the contest!"

Chapter 6

The Silvas got up early the next morning.

"I have a great day planned for you," Samuel said. "A lot of rivers flow into the Zambezi. There are many animals in them. We'll spend the day exploring."

"Whatever you say," Rafael said. "You're the expert."

They loaded two canoes into a truck. Some boxed lunches and other gear were packed too. They took off down a bumpy road.

"The Tutsi River flows into the Zambezi five miles from here. Twenty miles up the Tutsi there's a waterfall," Samuel said. "We'll put the canoes into the water by the falls. Then we'll paddle back to the lodge."

"That's sounds far. How long will it take us?" Lilia asked.

"It depends how much we stop," Samuel replied. "But we'll be on the river all day."

The road was just a jungle path. The Tutsi River was big. And the pool below the falls was deep.

Samuel sat in the back of the first canoe. Franco was in the front. And Lilia sat in the middle. Rafael, Ana, and Antonio took the second canoe.

The Silvas saw some amazing life on the riverbanks. Gazelles, impalas, and zebras came to the river for water. Crocodiles lay in the sun on the shore. Hippos eyed the canoes with little interest. All the Silvas took pictures. Even Antonio finally got some shots.

About twenty minutes later, they came to a little island. Samuel and the Silvas ate lunch there. It was hot under the African sun.

"It's almost three o'clock. We're still eight miles from the Zambezi," Samuel said. "Let's get a move on."

A mile downstream the river widened. The two canoes fit side by side. Then suddenly the river seemed to explode.

Everyone screamed. A gigantic hippo jumped out of the water! It bit the back of a canoe. The boat fell apart. Lilia and Franco were thrown into the water. Samuel cried out in pain. The huge hippo was biting his leg!

Rafael had no time to think. The two-thousand-pound hippo crashed into the second canoe. Now Antonio and his parents were also in the water. Scared by all of the people, the hippo let go of Samuel's leg. It went back under the water.

Ana saw a sandbar in the river. They swam over. Samuel was hurt.

His leg was bleeding. Rafael looked around. It was not good.

All the supplies were gone. And they were miles away from help. Someone from the lodge would come look for them. But it would be hours before anyone knew they were missing.

They were stuck in middle of the river. Wild animals were all around them.

"How are you doing?" Rafael asked Samuel.

Samuel looked up and shook his head.

"I've been traveling this river eight years," Samuel said. "Nothing like this has ever happened. I don't know why that hippo attacked us."

"Let's not worry about that now," Rafael said. "We have crocodiles to worry about."

"You're right, Rafael," said Samuel. "The crocodiles will know we are trapped out here. Do we have any canoe paddles?"

"No. We lost everything," Rafael replied.

"Keep an eye out for any branches floating in the river," Samuel said. "It doesn't take much to fend off hungry crocs. But we need something."

Chapter 7

Lilia was wet, tired, and scared.
"Do you think we'll be okay?" Lilia
asked.

"Of course we will," Rafael said.
"People at the lodge will know we
are missing. We'll be rescued soon
enough. We have to stay calm. Keep
a clear head."

"But what about the crocodiles?"
Lilia asked.

"We can keep them away," Rafael said. "There are six of us here. We'll fight them off."

But Rafael wasn't sure he was telling Lilia the truth. The crocs would become more aggressive when it got dark. Keeping them off the little sandbar would be very hard.

Franco and Antonio stood on the edge of the sandbar. They looked for anything they could use as weapons. Lilia and Ana found some rocks. There were already some big crocodiles swimming around the sandbar. More would come soon.

Just before dark Franco saw something in the water. He thought it was another crocodile. But it wasn't! It was a tree branch. The branch was moving fast. Someone would have to swim past the crocs to get it. Franco didn't think. He dove into the water and grabbed the branch. Then he swam back. But Franco didn't know that a crocodile was right behind him!

Rafael and Antonio threw rocks at the crocodile. One landed on top of the croc's head. It must have hurt it. The croc stopped chasing Franco.

"Good work, Franco," Rafael said. "This branch will help keep the crocs away."

All they could do was wait. The Silvas formed a circle around Samuel. They only had a branch and rocks as weapons. At least fifteen crocodiles surrounded them. Then the sun went down. Everything went dark.

Rafael swung a branch at the crocs over and over. Each time one croc backed off, another one appeared.

The branch was heavy. Rafael's arms hurt. He gave it to Franco and took a rest. Antonio threw some rocks at the crocodiles. There were only a few rocks left.

Soon it was midnight. Everyone heard a boat. The Silvas yelled out. The boat got to the sandbar just in time. The rocks were all gone. The branch was broken. When the boat came, the crocs swam away. The Silvas escaped danger in Africa once again!

Chapter 8

The Silvas only had one day left
in Africa. Since Samuel was in the
hospital, they got a new guide. His
name was Kasim.

"Nothing like this has ever
happened before," Kasim said.

"We know that wild animals are
unpredictable," Rafael said. "If we
wanted to see them safely, we would
have gone to a zoo."

"Good point," Kasim said. "But after yesterday, why don't we look at animals from a powerboat? It's the safest way to travel the Zambezi."

The powerboat was perfect. Everyone felt very safe. It was a great way to travel on the river.

Kasim took them to a big cove. A herd of Cape buffalo was on the shore. Kasim shut off the engine. The boat drifted toward shore. The Silvas took pictures of the big buffalos. Crocs were all around them. But the Silvas didn't care. They were safe inside the powerboat.

It was a fun and peaceful day. It was just what the Silvas wanted!

Chapter 9

The Silvas' African safari was over.
They flew back to Boston. They
traveled for twenty hours. Everyone
was happy to finally be home in the
Heights.

The next day Ana got three
envelopes. She wrote a name on
each one.

"Print out your pictures from the
safari," Ana said. "Put your five best

shots in your envelope. Next week Maya and Emilio Brown are coming over. They own an art gallery in town. They are going to judge your pictures."

Everyone was excited.

Antonio looked through his pictures. He thought he had a good one. But he didn't know if it was good enough to win. Lilia and Franco wouldn't stop making fun of him for messing up so many pictures. Winning would keep them quiet.

Chapter 10

The Browns came over for dinner.
After the meal, the Browns took
the safari pictures into the family
room. An hour later they had a
winner.

"There're some great shots here,"
Maya said.

She pulled out one of Lilia's
pictures. It was of a lioness attacking
a wildebeest.

"This is one of my favorites," Maya said. "But there's one that is even better."

Maya tossed the winning photo onto the table.

"Antonio is the winner!" Emilio exclaimed.

"No way!" Lilia cried.

The Silvas stared at Antonio's picture. It showed a big crocodile chasing Ana. Rafael was standing over the croc holding a tree branch. He was about to hit it over the head. The picture really captured the terrifying experience on the sandbar.

Antonio was clearly the winner. None of the Silvas argued with the Browns' choice.

"Antonio, you must have nerves of steel to take that photo," Emilio said. "It's amazing that you took it with all of the action on the sandbar."

"Well," Antonio sighed. "It was just dumb luck. When I pointed the camera, the crocs started attacking. I wasn't sure I even took the picture until later."

"Congratulations, Antonio," Ana said, giving him a hug. "You get to choose the location of our next family vacation!"

Lilia frowned. "Wow, Antonio. Don't choose anything too crazy. It's hardly fair that your accidental picture won the contest," she pouted. "Just kidding," Lilia said with a smile.

"Another trip to Africa is out," sighed Antonio. "I just want to stay close to home. No more crocs for me!"